BRAIN TALES
Volume One

First Edition
ISBN 978-0-9811592-0-1

Published by:
ProSpec Industries Inc
PO Box 25100
Moncton, New Brunswick
E1C 9M9
Canada
http://www.ProSpecIndustries.com

ProSpec Industries Inc books are available at special discounts for bulk purchases for sales promotions, fundraising, or educational use. Special editions or book excerpts can also be created to specification upon request.

For more information about the author, Sarah Butland, please visit: http://www.SarahButland.com

With many thanks to Trent and Elba Washburn for putting up with my changes and deadlines. Trent, your work is very impressive and I look forward to working with you in the future.

Also a huge thank you to my publisher, my husband, my soulmate for all of his patience and effort.

Contents

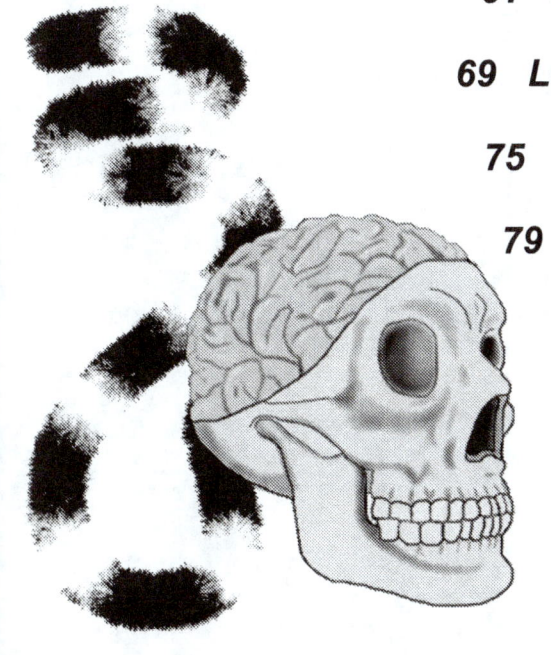

There he stood. Like the light at the end of a tunnel, he was there. Almost as if I died and had gone to heaven. I wasn't even looking for salvation, but he was ready to give it, which left me no choice but to accept.

I was blinded by what was in front of me. It took a few moments for my sight to adjust from the darkness that surrounded me, and when it finally did, I wasn't ready. I stumbled, almost falling into him, but he was ready and he broke my fall. His arms felt strong, but I quickly got up from them. Putting my full weight on my own shoes again, I felt much more independent. Much more like myself.

As my eyes focused, I saw a young man who looked to be about my own age but with experience that I didn't have. He wore faded jeans with an old t-shirt. His sneakers were worn and tattered. This look was what brought me back down to earth; at least for a little while. I never saw him before, but it was a university town and I didn't know everyone.

"Are you okay?" he asked. I couldn't help but answer, "yes" even though I felt as if I was still falling. His appearance wasn't stencil perfect, but I was never concerned with what others thought. He was an unexpected relief after I had spent an hour and a half watching an awful movie. A reprieve from being so worried about the school paper I hadn't started.

"Thanks," I mumbled. "I just... I couldn't see very well. Everything is so bright out here compared to in there. I guess I should wait here until my sight adjusts. Wouldn't want you to have to jump into traffic to save me from falling; it's much safer to play hero on the sidewalk."

"Thanks for the warning and the compliment. I'm just going in and wouldn't want to look like a fool. I'll wait for my eyes to adjust to the darkness at the entrance before I stumble myself. There might not be someone inside to catch me."

"So! I'm a fool? Thank you, nice to meet you, too." I pretended to be disinterested in continuing the conversation and turned to walk away. He stopped me with, "Sorry, I didn't mean that. Oh, I'm always doing this when I meet a beautiful woman. My heart beats much faster than my brain."

I turned back, startled by his honesty as

well as his compliment. "Apology accepted." I was being so forgiving and yet so harsh. I began feeling as if I was under a microscope and he was the scientist.

After a speechless, awkward moment, we both spoke at once. He asked how the movie was, and I said, "I should go," despite my wanting to stay. "It was a lot of senseless violence, wasn't really what I expected. I was going to write a report on it for school but didn't get much inspiration from it. I guess I'll have to change my project idea."

"Well, thanks for that tip, too. I think I'll save the money and find some other way to spend my afternoon. Any suggestions?"

He was unbelievable. He was actually listening to what I was saying and heeding my advice. I was always on an active search for a gentleman, and just when I called it off and decided to go solo, he was waiting. Just waiting for me to stumble on him. He was waiting for an answer, oh what did he ask me? Oh, for suggestions on what to do with his afternoon. "I don't know. What do you like doing?"

"I'm finding it hard to find anything I like. I'm new in town and don't really know anyone around besides my sister, and I'm getting pretty sick of her. I'm hoping for some ideas on where to go to meet people. Have any? You look like a popular woman."

I took a risk, the first one in my life, and I didn't have time to think through the consequences. It just came out. "I was headed to a small get together with friends, actually. She has a pool, and we were going to grab stuff for a barbecue. You're welcome to join us."

"Man, I love swimming. Are you sure your friend won't mind? Oh, no, I don't have swimming shorts! Guess not, any more ideas?" He looked truly disappointed, and I already cared so much about this stranger that I couldn't just leave him stranded.

"There's a mall just a block from her place. I have to stop and pick up a few things anyway. It's no trouble at all if you want to run in and pick something out."

The light in his eyes returned and a soft smile appeared on his face. "Would you take "no" for an answer?"

"Not after hearing your desperate plea," I joked nonchalantly. Truth was, I wasn't going to let him miss out partly because my friends wouldn't believe I asked and because I wanted to learn more about him. "Come on. It'll be fun."

We left – he following in his car, not knowing where to go, and I getting on the cell phone to warn Jenny of a previously uninvited guest. She was shocked that I was inviting a stranger over, but no one was as shocked as I once I realized that that's exactly what I did. But I couldn't get his vibrancy out of my mind, no matter how loud I turned up the volume on the stereo. After a few glances in the rearview mirror, we arrived.

We parked close together and walked inside with few words between us. Once we reached the doors, I pointed to a men's clothing store and guaranteed him that he would find something there for a good price and that I'd be back in a minute. He smiled the most stunning smile, and we parted.

I picked up a few things to avoid his realizing that I was lying. I knew a get together could always use wine, cheese, crackers, and salad. I tried getting some that he would like but realized that I barely even knew him and didn't know if he even drank wine. I wanted to learn. On the way out I decided to rent a few new releases as a nightcap for the get together.

I got back just as he was making his purchase and realized that I let out a sigh of relief when I saw that he was still there. I asked if he found what he needed, and he told me that he found more than what he was looking for. I didn't realize what that meant until years later.

He saw the wine and approved. He admitted that he never enjoyed a barbecue unless you could have some snacks while the food was cooking. It took so long and smelled so good that it made him hungry, so he was glad I bought some. It seemed as if I knew him before we ever met.

Leaving the mall, we again said very little. It felt as if we didn't need to say much, but that we both had a lot to say. The silence left us to our own thoughts, but it wasn't awkward as this was a moment to reflect. Getting into our separate cars, I asked if he needed to make any other stops before the party. He told me that he was all set and excited to get in the pool. We were off.

We arrived at Jenny's after everyone else was settled in. Everyone was still out lounging in their suits when we reached the backyard and the guests looked and were shocked at our arrival. "Hey Suzi, who's your friend?" It was at that point that I realized how insensible and insensitive I was really being when I couldn't recall his name. I quickly realized it was because I had nothing to recall. "Oh, I'm so embarrassed," I said turning to my guest. "I'm Suzi and you are…"

"No need to be embarrassed, Suzi. This is the first I heard of your name. I'm Andrew Stewart, but please, call me Andy." He succeeded at making me feel a tad bit better about not getting his name. It was such a different meet that neither of us thought to ask.

"Everyone, this is Andy. Andy this is Jenny; she lives here. And this is her boyfriend, Thomas. This is Eric, Tori, Elizabeth, and Sasha. We all go to the same college together. When we're not studying, we're usually here."

After making small talk with everyone, Andy offered to start up the barbecue. Everyone was ecstatic with the idea as we were all very hungry but extremely hot and wanting to swim. He suggested we take a dip in the pool after taking our orders on how we liked our steak and potatoes. I told him that I just wanted a simple hamburger, not being much into steaks.

Everyone else chose the steaks. I couldn't believe how helpful he was after I saw that he got everything on to cook. I suggested that he go in to change into his shorts and jump on in.

He accepted, and in moments he appeared like a Hollywood star at the doorway. The swimming trunks he picked out were the same blue as his eyes, which accentuated his tanned body. His hair slicked back and his six abs were almost visible. My heart stopped for the second time that day. When fully clothed he wasn't obviously gorgeous. In swimming trunks he was positively desirable. Feeling as if I was staring, I dove into the water to avoid discussion.

He swam like a dolphin and played water games like a pro. It was hard to keep up. There were a few instances where we ended up so close to each other, it seemed as if the water parted. These moments were awkward for the other guests but seemed natural to me. Although we ended them almost before they started to avoid future questioning, they revived my energy level. But we all had a good time, and when the smells of the barbecue were too much, we all got out of the pool. I offered to help Andy set up for supper while everyone talked amongst themselves.

Inside and away from everyone, Andy poured a glass of wine. He had checked the steaks, concluding that they needed a few more minutes on the barbecue. My hamburger was done. I brought some crackers and cheese along with the rest of the bottle of wine out to the other guests. I excused myself and returned inside. Andy was still setting the table, and I helped him finish. He asked me why I didn't have a steak.

"They just seem like so much work to eat. I like simple, easy to handle food. Not to mention it's easier on the chef."

"I wouldn't have minded, really. Everyone else is having steak, so it wouldn't have taken any longer."

"The truth is I'm fussy about how well a steak is cooked. If there was the least bit of pink in it, I couldn't eat it, but I wouldn't want to insult you. And I like a good burger just as well." He seemed satisfied with my answer, complimented me on the wine selection, and gave everyone the go ahead to come inside.

Everyone resumed talking like old friends and complimented the chef on his excellent work. We ate until we were too full to eat any more and had a wonderful time doing so. Everything was perfect. Andy fit right in with everyone as if he were one of the original crew. He explained that he was going to be starting school with us in the fall. He was our age, but he had taken some time off from schooling to explore the world. It was so interesting to hear about someone who was brave enough to do what everyone only dreamed of doing.

Andy was going into nursing in hopes of becoming a doctor. He planned to return to third-world countries to help the hopeless. Giving hope to the despair was Andy's wish. His worldly outlook melted my heart. I never thought there was any reason to doubt his tales.

As the sun was setting and our damp bodies were feeling the effects, Jenny invited us all into the living room for a nightcap. Everyone accepted. Jenny closed the screen door and prepared a tray with the remaining crackers and cheese.

When I stood up, a feeling of nausea came over me, which I tried to shrug off to falling so hard for this stranger, but it wouldn't be so simple. We changed out of our bathing suits and returned to the living room. I took the longest time. In the bathroom my head still spun, so I sat on the toilet while I dressed. My friends must have noticed my taking a long time, as they all turned to watch me emerge from the bathroom. When they asked me if anything was wrong, I replied as honestly as I could.

"I'm not feeling so hot. Must have been from being in the sun so long. I'll be fine."

"Could have fooled me," Andy responded but then caught himself. "I'm sorry to hear that." He reached his hand to my forehead and felt that I was in the beginnings of a fever. I convinced everyone that it was really nothing and to put in the movie. It was a good pick; no one had seen it yet.

Through the movie I felt drowsy and eventually fell asleep. Sitting next to Andy, I awoke after using his lap as a pillow. The movie was over. I began to complain that I didn't see it when I couldn't help but vomit. Unfortunately, this landed on Andy's lap where my head just lay. I felt too awful to feel embarrassed.

My friends helped me up and walked me to Jenny's bedroom. They called the emergency line regarding my symptoms, and my friends quickly decided to take me to the hospital. They woke me from my slumber, and Jenny offered to drive me. My other friends were going to follow in their own cars.

My first muddled thoughts were that I invited the wrong man into my heart again. For all I knew he preyed on idiots like me that would accept his lame story and then ask him to cook for me. In between my sudden vomiting sessions on the way to the hospital, Jenny tried to console me. She made attempts at convincing me that Andy wasn't all that bad. That he couldn't have done anything intentional to hurt me. I could hear doubt in her voice, and I wasn't convinced, knowing that she wasn't.

"Sorry to be the party pooper again. This time I was really trying to be open about everything. Stupid me! Always falling in love with strangers."

"Don't blame yourself, honey. Things might not be as they appear. You gave this guy a chance, and he blew it, but we did have fun. If this guy did anything bad, we will get him. And then we won't talk to him again."

She was trying to comfort me, and I was grateful, but inside I was tearing myself up. My physical appearance was showing how I felt inside. I would decide to never be so welcoming to a stranger again. I couldn't feel any more stupid than at that moment. I just knew he tried to poison me. Paranoia was at its best.

We arrived at the hospital, and I was admitted. I heard nurses saying that it might just be sunstroke, a party gone bad, or food poisoning. The party gone bad was right, but not in the way that the nurses implied. At the mention of food poisoning, I became even more convinced that Andy was wrong for me. I needed a man that could cook because I couldn't. And he had to be able to cook without making me sick. With that final thought behind me, thankfully I fell asleep.

Upon waking I felt a tiny bit better until I saw who was sitting in the chair by my bed. Andy was watching me. Through murky eyes I almost missed it, but Jenny was standing behind him, directing a tear down her cheek with her finger. What are friends for if not to point out things others are trying to hide? I looked back at Andy and saw that he was crying. He saw that I noticed and tried to casually wipe the lone tear resting on his chin. A man that cried but didn't want to be seen crying. It looked so fictitious. It seemed so staged. I certainly wasn't an actor looking for a cue. He wouldn't get away that easily.

"How are you?"

"Honestly, not so good. I'm dry. I need a drink," I mumbled to him still groggy from the fever. No sooner was it out of my mouth than Andy was pouring fresh ice water into a glass and holding it up to my mouth to drink from the straw. I took a drink and asked him why he was there. I let the water soothe my throat as I finished the glass.

"I feel so guilty. I am responsible for you being here. I guess my heart was beating so fast that it drowned my intelligence. I don't want to leave before I know that you are better. I can't leave until I know you're safe. Is there anything else I can get for you? Anything, anything at all, it's the least I could do."

"Not right now. Well, maybe a magazine from the gift shop, a woman's advice magazine would be fine." He left, and I took full advantage of the opportunity to talk with Jenny. "What's going on, Jenny? What is wrong with me?" At that point I was blaming myself for being so blind more than blaming anyone else.

"Emotionally – nothing but physically you have food poisoning. It's actually not him that should feel guilty. In fact, he's been quite the gentleman. Look, the hamburgers were bad before Andy even put them on the grill. I guess I forgot to put them in the fridge when I got home. I thought that it would be fine. I just got distracted when everyone came over. I talked to the doctor, and they told me that you'll be fine. I haven't built up the courage to tell anyone else yet. I just feel awful."

"So, Andy isn't bad? It may be the fever talking, but I thought he was evil and preying on me." I didn't care who did it, that it was an accident was what relieved me. I found it hard to believe what I was hearing but knew that I didn't see any pink in the burger. Then it hit me, if I told him that he wasn't responsible would Andy leave? Was this the last memory I was going to have of the man who swept me off my feet? Not to mention put me in bed, it didn't matter that it was a hospital bed. Andy didn't try to kill me.

"It seems like you made a good decision by inviting him. It's up to you, of course, but it sounds like this guy is the one you've been looking for." Andy entered acting as if he never had heard what Jenny said, and maybe he didn't, but it seemed like such perfect timing. He handed the magazine to me and sat back down. He looked from Jenny to me and commented on the silence.

I explained to him that he wasn't the guilty one and that it was actually Jenny who was responsible. I felt that it would be the right thing to do despite the risk. I heard him breathe a sigh of relief, but I couldn't keep my eyes open long enough to see if he still felt responsible. When I awoke again it was dark, but he was still sitting beside my bed.

I watched him struggle to sleep on the chair until he stirred, and then I asked him why he was still there. He was still dressed in the clothes he wore when I met him. It seemed like so long ago, but it was only the day before. He hadn't yet left the hospital. I explained that I was going to be fine and that he had no reason to feel guilty.

"I just wanted to spend the afternoon with you, but I'm not done getting to know you. I will be here until you are ready to go home."

I knew it was neither the medication nor the fever when my temperature rose this time; it was the smooth line that Andy fed me. At that time it almost felt scripted, a perfect thing to say to make himself look the hero. He promised that if given the opportunity, he would make everything up to me.

It would be a couple days before I got over the awful food poisoning. Andy was the one who drove me back to campus and then stayed with me until I was back to myself. It was the longest first date I ever had as well as the best. It was also the last first date I had, which made me love the movie I saw that day. He certainly made up for the bad night within those days. He never again mentioned my being sick on his lap and I certainly never brought it up.

I was blinded by love that day so long ago, and I was able to see much better since. The bright light that I stumbled upon in my days of despair was the same light that led the way to where I am today.

DREAMS DO COME TRUE

The clock sounded, interrupting my dreams, and "my" day began. Showered and dressed, the toilet called my name. I replied, but it was muted due to the needs of my young daughter. Flushing away thoughts of performing any forces of nature, I also decided I wouldn't have any time to do anything that came natural.

My attempts crawled back inside, and I tended to the needs of my offspring who, too, would take some time to perform. This deed is much like a person's thought process and, when it makes itself known, should be set free. Unfortunately, if it is not, you never know when it'll make its second appearance. When a young child has a movement and shares this with you, a mother should rejoice. Annoying as it is to be interrupted while creating a timeless piece, some performances do need to have an intermission; however inconvenient – during a movement or otherwise.

And so my day began, giving myself, my time and my sanity to others. Keeping everything inside of me that I started with and performing acts that seem to go unnoticed. My family, giving me reasons to do things, both natural and not, but borrowing on my time to commend them for doing acts on their own.

I became so consumed in other lives that were borne of me but are not me; not my life but live with me.

I was always a dreamer, always dreamt of a family with a loving husband, someone who would make sacrifices along with me. A husband who would support my weaknesses and strengths and give me time to work with both. That dream became a reality, even though he seems hard to recognize sometimes.

A twenty-four hour world does not leave me a whole lot of time to appreciate the play I chose to attend. Between working a dead-end job and looking after a family of four, time for me is limited. I wish I could say that because I'm not alone in this life it is made easier, but because I use the written word to escape or dwell, whichever my soul may need, I cannot write or say.

I pricked myself with the safety pin I poked through my daughter's diaper and I was oblivious to the blood until my daughter was dressed. During the process I somehow managed to wipe a red stream across my forehead and my brand new blouse. I waited for Trisha's babysitter to arrive and then I escaped to the bathroom to re-shower and redress. During the mundane process, I checked my watch to see that I was already fifteen minutes late for work. I stopped the process, ran to my bedroom, grabbed the phone, and dialed the number to my office.

While listening to the elevator music, I wandered out to the living room where Trisha was entertaining her adoring sitter. I stood where I couldn't be seen and watched as my daughter quickly recited the alphabet and all the nursery rhymes I ever heard and ones that I haven't. These were sung so sweetly and with such adorable actions that my mind was brought from my aching abdomen to the graceful performance. I don't know how long I was listening to my manager who replaced elevator music, but it was long enough for him to become annoyed.

"Sorry, I was… nevermind. It's Christine Slyder, and I'm calling to advise you that I won't be coming in today or ever again for that matter."

"Why don't you take some time off to think

about it?"

"I've thought about it for five years, Mr Branson. It's time I do something for myself and this is it."

"If there's no way for me to change your mind, then I'll wish you luck. I will not be able to hold your position for very long…"

"I wouldn't expect you to," I said and hung up. I went back to the bedroom and changed into ratty clothes, returned to the living room and made an announcement.

"I'm staying home today, so if you want to go, feel free, but I'm not kicking you out." I didn't want to explain the extent of my staying home until I talked with the entire family to know if we could afford keeping her.

"If you don't mind I would like to go home. My mother isn't feeling the best today. But I'll stay as long as you need."

"By all means, get out of here. Did you need a drive home?"

"I biked here, so I'll be fine, thank you though." She was out of the house before I could even think of something more to say, and I was surrounded in confusion – where a four year old spends most of her life.

I sat down beside her and played until she complained of hunger. Then I had her help me prepare lunch. As soon as we finished, we went outside for a walk. It was soon time for Tommy to return and Trisha was showing signs of exhaustion. So I took her home and put her down for a nap.

During her nap I was able to put together a hearty meal and clean the house from top to bottom. When Tommy entered, Trisha woke up and we all played hide and seek for a while. When my husband arrived home, the children were quiet from exhaustion and the table was set with his favourite meal. I waited until everyone's stomachs were full and then made my announcement.

"I'm happy for you, dear, but I wish you would have waited to talk to me."

"I can go back to work if we can't afford it, but I'm not going back to that place."

"I'm joking, honey. I just got a raise today, so it'll work out wonderfully."

The kids were excited too, obvious by the smiles on their faces while they slept. My husband helped me put them to bed, and then we went to bed. I went exhausted from the lives I lived, knowing that my life was now my own. With a stomach full of music and food, I drifted to sleep with nursery rhymes reciting in my ears.

I slept peacefully through the night and woke up two hours earlier than normal, feeling fresh and alive. I left my husband to go to the bathroom where I was able to rid myself of leftover pieces and then compose the first piece of material in years. I was out of the bathroom before anyone could interrupt and sat down at the desktop and began to type what was already completed in my head.

AT EASE

It was a small box, but I was still so far away that my judgment could not possibly be considered accurate; even the trees surrounding it looked distorted. I trotted on trying to ignore the ever increasing volume of the nearby river but finding it impossible. Turning around to see the rest of the road crew working so far away made me almost regret beginning the long road to the outhouse, but the other choice would be much more detrimental as the new guy. Besides, I was almost half way to my destination, so I couldn't let myself give up.

My feet were already tired and swelling from working since six am, but they seemed to know that it was about time I sit down even though the duration would be so short. The box was growing much like the tiny facecloth my son immersed in water and watched swell to regular size. There were several times on my journey that I almost had myself convinced to just go behind a tree, like the crew suggested; the road had yet to be driven so there was no risk of being seen, but the outhouse would give me the proper materials necessary for my operation. It would also be an excuse as to why I took so long with my break.

I briefly considered using leaves to wipe my eyes, but I wanted no trace of the process, so I chose to walk the mile to clear my head. Besides, the immediate forest consisted of a lot more evergreen than hardwood trees. I paused and peered into the forest, recalling how my little Sandy loved climbing the evergreens on our land. Whenever I had a moment to spend with my son, he would choose to be climbing a tree. I built him a tree house that still remained standing even though Sandy would never again spend a night camping out amongst the trees.

I continued moving without even realizing I was doing so and was at my destination before I stopped seeing the tree house. Frustrated that I didn't remember to bring a mirror, I furiously wiped at my eyes with the paper the outhouse offered which, unfortunately, was only a smidgen smoother than a leaf would have been.

The once expanding stream running down my cheeks slowed, then ceased after many attempts of my heart, and I left the outhouse with a much clearer head. This time when I heard the river, it gave me the thought of checking my reflection in its waters to ensure I wouldn't be the laughing stock of the crew. Stumbling through the trees, I recalled how Sandy decided to be an environmentalist after his summer of planting trees for a local company.

Reaching the river bend, I stretched my neck outward so my head was above the water and was surprised to see my son looking back at me. Even though I just cried a gallon or so of tears, I found an ocean more reserved somewhere inside me. Once the tears reached the river, the reflection distorted and then reshaped as my own. The moment of confusion was enough to clear my head as I realized that even though he was watching from above, Sandy could still not be proud of me.

Since my son's passing, I was making my living cutting down almost the same amount of trees that my son planted. The trees sent a small breeze across the water, and I knew it contained a blessing from my only child. I also realized that I could no longer cut down the trees but would build roads around them.

I almost decided to walk all the way home, past the outhouse instead of back to the crew, but I didn't want to worry them. Besides, my feet refused to walk any more than they had to, and my vehicle was waiting for me there. I approached the group with my speech already in mind and spoke it with no interruptions, from the audience or my ever-flowing tears. I no longer cared what my former coworkers thought; I was going to make my Sandy proud. Before anyone could object, I was in my car, destined for home.

Upon arriving I saw that my wife's car was in the driveway, but when I went into the house, she was nowhere to be found. I wandered out to Sandy's tree house, a place I intentionally avoided since his death but where I finally located my wife. Her legs were dangling out of the cabin's door, as if she were awaiting my arrival. There was no doubt in my mind that she knew I'd be there.

"You're home early," she said first.

"And I could say the same for you."

"I know, and you're going to think I'm crazy if you ask why. Assuming that it's the same for you, I'm not going to ask. Need help up? I can tell you I had a hard time up that rope and wished all the way up that Sandy let you build him a ladder."

"I'm just amazed he let me use the wood needed for the cabin."

"Me, too." When I was up and comfortable, she asked, "why did he have to go, John, he was so young?" Her tears weren't anything we had control over, so we had to let them shed. My reservoir was dry, so I expressed my madness by hitting the wall which knocked down the lone picture hanging in the cabin. Sarah and I sat staring at our family, hugging a tree but seeing different memories flash by the glass. In a fit of rage I threw the object at the wall and watched it smash into hundreds of shards, only among the bits of glass flew paper and bills. Sarah was the first to begin gathering the bills in a state of confusion, but I saw the note before she did.

Mom, Dad:

If you've found this, I'm sure I am on a mission somewhere trying to save the world from pollution and you finally decided to tear down my old tree house. I've had a lot of good memories in that cabin to keep me happy for years to come and for that I'm grateful.
The money isn't much, but it was all I could do. I know you were having trouble years ago even though you tried to hide it from me. If you

sell that big house of yours, I'm sure both of you will be set and won't have to work again. If I ever visit, I'll be fine on a couch or in a sleeping bag on the floor. If I don't come back, I am sorry but know that I'm safe and in a good place.

Keep each other warm and happy and remember me every time you see a tree.

Love with all of me,

Sandy Harrison

PS: Wherever I'll be in the future, know that I'll be happy if I see the trees.

From somewhere deep down inside, I found even more tears and shed them as my wife shed hers. I don't know how long we stayed there in almost complete silence, but the sun set by the time the silence was broken. "How much is there?"

"I haven't kept track." When we counted the bills, there was over $6000 once stuffed behind our family's favourite picture. "It must be all the money he made planting trees. Oh, he was such a smart boy when it came to spending – or not spending – money. What do you think?"

"I think he was smart about everything, and we'd be stupid not to listen to him. I do refuse to take down the cabin, however, as the new owners may have a tenant for it. We will take the rope with us, though, and find a use for it in our new house. Ready to go back down, Sarah?"

"In a minute, John, in a minute."

"I'll have an egg-white omelet with a side of sausage, drowned in maple syrup. And a beer, if you've got one." He replied quietly, politely, but she was still offended, even though she was the one who offered.

"Do you think this is a restaurant? I don't get paid enough to serve the people around here, stranger or not. I pity your situation. No one deserves to have their car break down in the middle of a storm, but I am not a maid." While she was saying her speech, however, Jennifer was preparing everything for the man of the night, even to the point of pouring the beer into a freezer mug. Obviously, this was a sensitive subject for Brock's host and one that he'd try to avoid.

Their introduction was strained as Jennifer was cautious about letting him in, but as she stood with the door open, the wind chilled her to the bone so she asked him to come in. He told her his name was Brock as he pointed to his broken-down car stuck in the snow. She did offer a meal but only after he complained profusely of being so hungry and not being able to stop to eat on his long drive. While she finished preparing his meal, he escaped to the little boy's room and relieved just a minute amount of his stress.

He returned and drank the beer back before Jennifer had the opportunity to change her mind. He was still waiting for the eggs and sausage when he saw flashing lights through the kitchen window and stood to investigate. By the time Brock adorned his boots, jacket, and hat and opened the door, the tow truck was already on its way with his car. "Damn," he shouted at the snow. Jennifer was used to growing up in a household of males so knew there was something more bothering Brock but decided against prying.

On his way back in, Brock adorned his most apologetic look and, once undressed of his winter attire told his hostess: "They got my car. I'm not going anywhere 'til the snow clears. I promise not to be a hassle and to clean-up after myself. I have money in my car; I'll reimburse you for the night. Anything you want, Jennifer."

She wasn't pleased but tried to tell him otherwise. "I guess it'll be good to have another man around. Thomas will be home tonight and can take you in to town in the morning."

"Ma'am, I don't think anyone is coming home tonight…"

"You'd be surprised at how well my husband drives; he was the man who just took your car to his lot. He'll be home."

"It was… you own…he took…" the question couldn't fully form in his head and was surprised that he could spit out the words he did.

"Yes, yes, and yes. Tom would be doing his job, which he does very well. The road would need to be cleared for any other fool trying to make it somewhere."

Brock realized that was an insult meant solely for him, but he forced himself to ignore it. He sat and ate, without complaint, only glancing at the busy body briefly and occasionally. She was stunning in her special hardened way, and she seemed to know it, so he decided not to make mention of it. He wouldn't bring anything up that could result in a scene that took any more energy out of him or her. They were both in an unwelcomed situation, and he would be the one without a home – if it became unbearable.

Brock stood and placed his empty plate in the sink, ran the water, and asked for the dish soap. "There's no need to fill the sink for only a few dishes. Turn the water off, and we'll wait for Tom to return. I'm sure he'll be ravenous after such a busy day."

"Is there anything else I can do to help then? It's really the least I could do; I'm sure he'll be unimpressed by my intrusion."

"Why don't you go out and bring in some more wood; that way Tom won't have to when he returns." She gave Brock the directions while he put his outer clothing on, and he was on his way. While trudging through the snow, Brock was slightly surprised to see fresh footprints in the snow, which were pointing towards the house. He thought about following them but decided against it when he saw the pile of wood he was after. He would come back once he started the fire.

Upon entering the house, Brock realized he made the right decision. The culprit of the footprints was standing right in front of him. Jennifer told him about her children, but he stupidly expected they were in school and, instead, they were taking full advantage of their day off. Before introductions could be made, the door opened behind him and he was knocked unconscious.

When Brock came to, he was lying, fully dressed and completely soaked on a bed surrounded by strangers. Slowly the faces began to be familiar to Brock, but only two came back to him as he struggled to make sense of his position. The smell of chocolate chip cookies invaded his senses and he asked Jennifer if he could have some.

Laughter came at Brock's answer, which only helped confuse him more. The man began blubbering an apology, and Brock realized it was Jennifer's husband and the man who hit him from behind confused as to why a stranger was on his territory. "How long have I been out?"

One of the sons answered, "about an hour."

"Have you all been watching me the entire time?"

A familiar voice, "one of us has, but the rest have been eating. I made extra for you. I hope you like chili."

"Anything at this point will be terrific. Why did you do that to me? A man is already down on his luck, and you have to sucker punch him?"

"I'm sorry, sir. There have been a slew of robberies around these parts, and we're all on edge. I was protecting my family; I hope you can understand that. I'm Tom." Brock sat up and offered a hand that was shaken strongly by Tom.

"Oh, and Brock, your money isn't accepted here; we'll call it even."

"I can understand, in fact it's my family bringing me to this area, so I do understand but the bump on my head will take a bit longer to get used to the idea."

"Yeah, sorry about that." Everyone helped Brock up and to the kitchen where he ate as much as he could fit inside him. The power went out while he was in bed, and he ate barely warm but still delicious chili by candlelight and in almost complete silence. The family welcomed him into the living room, where they gave him some of Tom's dry clothes which he changed into and then returned to sit by the fire.

The children were both sound asleep under blankets on the floor, but Tom and Jennifer were still wide awake. Brock realized that this was the perfect setting for a life-altering confession and hoped that he wouldn't be privy to one that night. Unfortunately, and fortunately, that wouldn't be the case.

As soon as Brock made himself

comfortable, Jennifer and Tom began asking questions which quickly changed how comfortable he was.

"What brought you to Diorville? Why now – in the middle of a major snowstorm? Where did you come from?"

"I'll start at the beginning and, hopefully, answer all of your questions. My son is ill and we've been trying everything to make him better. Unfortunately, the doctors will only be able to give a life expectancy if he gets a kidney transplant. His blood type and specifications can only be matched by a family member. We tested everyone we knew, and we're not an exact match to him. My wife and I have spent the last few months trying to find a long lost sibling, which brings me to Diorville." The story continued, and the Lewises listened intently and sympathetically. They let Brock finish before they made any comments, but when Jennifer spoke, the life altering moment began.

Jennifer shared a look with her husband that Brock wrongfully recognized as doubt but was in fact disbelief. She was speechless, trying to figure out the best way to phrase what she had to say, but as Brock looked on, she decided it best just to say it.

"Oh my God, I think you're my brother!"

The world took on a different look for Brock at that instant as he cursed himself for hating the situation he found himself in only minutes earlier. He was surprised to see the snow come to a slow halt and the clock on the stove come to light while the rest of the house remained lit by the glow of the fire. Jennifer and Brock sat so still while Tom retrieved some of his wife's baby pictures. When Brock saw the resemblance, he couldn't help but be hopeful but still fought the urge to believe.

"Did you want to call your son?"

"I can't. I mean, I want to be sure before I get everyone's hopes up and, besides, I haven't asked you yet if you would be willing to do this for me."

"Brock, I'd really have no choice if this is what we think it is."

"You do have a choice, although I have no choice but to ask you, beg you, to do this for my son."

"Of course."

Everyone in the house slept peacefully that night and awoke to Jennifer making French toast with maple syrup, bacon, and fresh orange juice. Brock found it to be the most delicious meal he'd ever eaten but was surprised at the silence of the family. He decided it was due to the fact that the boys didn't know about their discovery last night.

"When you're done, I'll take you in to get your truck so you can get back on the road. Jennifer needs to get a few things in town, too, so she'll be coming in with us."

"Sure. Looks like the weather is staying away now, which is fine by me. Looks like you boys will be back to school tomorrow."

Groans were his response.

In the truck Jennifer explained that the boys didn't know about her being adopted yet and she didn't want them to find out like this. If it was proven that they were related, she would tell them as she would want Brock and his family to be in their lives.

Before dropping off Brock to pick up his truck, Tom drove them to the nearest hospital for blood work. It would take a week for the results to come in as to whether or not she'd be suitable for Brock's son, but the initial results would be almost immediate. After spending some time in

47

town, Brock followed the husband and wife back to their house with his truck, and there was already a message waiting from Jennifer's doctor. Brock and Jennifer were brother and sister.

The celebration was a small one, as they still weren't sure if she'd be a match for Scott, Brock's son. At supper that night, Jennifer told her children the news and let them know Brock would be staying with them for a couple of days. Brock finally called home and told his wife that he found his sister but told her to keep it from Scott and the doctors until they knew the final results. Jennifer could feel the anticipation through the phone and in Brock's voice.

She prayed that night; they all did, and they prayed the next night and the next until the morning they woke to the sound of a fax coming in. The results were in and copied to Brock, his son's doctors and his wife. Jennifer and her family, Brock read the results; Tom and his children remained silent while both Jennifer and Brock took a seat and began to weep.

THE DESTINED BRAWL

The air was filled with the musty smell of cigarette smoke and the noise of drunken laughter. Miss Candlier attempted once again to drown out their gossip and accusation with her piano playing, but failed. And as she played, her mind wandered.

She was Mrs. Martin, and she no longer needed to play the piano in local bars for her husband was rich and offered her everything she never had. She and her husband waltzed around their bedroom without a care in the world. This was the life she dreamed of, one of happiness and luck, of traveling, and owning her own horse.

Miss Candlier was brought back to reality with a song request. "Miss, can you play 'Greensleeves'?" he slurred and off her hands went playing for the gentleman. Her mind began to slip into a more fulfilling state but was jarred by the brutal reality of a gunshot that sent her bolting upright on the piano bench, her hands continuing to play, despite her disapproval.

Miss Candlier's hands played on until the brawl became unbearably loud and disturbing. She couldn't work in this atmosphere anymore and stood from the bench with all intentions of retrieving her coat and hat. She never made it to the coat rack, which was only feet away. She tripped over one of the collecting dead bodies as a result of the brawl, and landed on her face, crushing her nose.

In her state of unconsciousness, Miss Candlier was stepped on, tripped over, kicked, and ignored, which wasn't much different from that of her state of consciousness. The fight broiled on and the bar was made the site of the biggest, most pointless brawl in the West of '58. Chairs were thrown and burned, people were thrown, killed, set on fire, and all because some drunken man, named Mr. Wesley "Temper" Barnes, lost the game of cards that was making his night. Unfortunately for Mr. Barnes, losing the game wasn't the worst of his troubles for that night was his last. In fact, Mr. Barnes was one of the first killed and was the man that Miss Candlier tripped over.

The fight was being moved outside just as Miss Candlier became aware of her whereabouts. She wasn't alone in the bar. A male occupant, who was surprisingly sober, came to her rescue. Over her bruised nose she recognized him as Doctor Martin and could feel her cheeks redden as she recalled her fantasy.

"That was quite a fall, Miss. Are you okay?" he questioned as he touched Miss Candlier's nose with his tender hand.

"Yes, I'm sure I'll be fine. Thank you, Dr. Martin," she replied as she tried to stand but was destined for the floor and fell. This time Dr. Martin's arms broke her fall and she fainted.

Dr. Martin brought the woman to his house to treat her for a broken nose and to give her a cup of tea. Miss Candlier expressed her gratitude and asked his accompaniment for dinner that night. He accepted and walked her home through the falling snow and dying men, protecting her from the gunshots that endangered the lives of everyone on the street.

Once home and away from harm, Miss Candlier began to prepare dinner as Dr. Martin set the table for the two. The table was complete with candles when Dr. Martin requested his hostess to play a tune on the piano in the next room. Reluctantly, Miss Candlier left her place at the stove and headed toward the piano, the selection of songs she knew sorting in her head. At the piano the pianist began to play "I Want to

Be Wanted," and surprisingly her host began to sing the words. They stopped only to eat, played until the middle of the night and then retired to their homes; Miss Candlier retired to her room.

The duet began gathering nightly and decided to take their show on the road. One night, in a room they rented above a bar, Dr. Martin played a record and danced with Mrs. Martin to the song. They waltzed around the room, not a care in the world.

The former Miss Candlier's fantasies came true.

PEELING APPLES

Some of us grow old with grace. Others, like me, have aged with nothing more than a few wrinkles. Each of which concealed a cherished, or not so cherished, memory. Some of these memories rather sketchy. A lot couldn't be forgotten no matter how hard we tried, but others were what made us unique. It was these events that we liked to repeat.

My most significant and deepest wrinkle came on the day that I discovered that I was old. My daughter approached me while I was baking.

"Mom, what are you making?"

"Pie, Dear, apple pie. I'll send some home with you so Richard has a taste."

"But, mom, where are the apples?"

I was defeated and couldn't hide my embarrassment. I felt the wrinkle invade my forehead, ever deeper with each beep from the stove and each glance from my daughter.

Taking the empty pie out of the oven, I was asked to sit.

"Mom, Richard and I have been talking and interviewing homes but before you object know that it's been hard on us, too. We can't find anything that would suit you, but we are not giving up."

"You know what's best for me, which is what I've always taught you. You make me so proud."

"You're not upset?"

"You said you haven't found a place yet so there's no reason to start peeling my oranges now."

"Don't you mean apples?"

"Oh, you wouldn't understand. Would you like a piece?"

"Mother, a piece of what? I'll pass on the pie shell."

My wrinkle stretched.

Touching it up with foundation I was able to conceal it for weeks; I wasn't able to conceal my aging.

When I remembered to go to bingo my friends seemed very confused. Their going senile startled me as we were always so close in age, but now the gap was so large. I thought it was the age gap that was widening; it was my wrinkle.

I never did win bingo. I may have, but I never saw the winnings. It didn't bother me if someone were taking it; I always gave to charities anyway.

It wasn't long before my daughter came to visit, this time with her husband.

"Hi, mom. Richard picked me up after work. We need to talk."

"That's nice, dear; I always enjoy talking to you. Oh, Richard, you came, too. How nice of you."

Julie raised her voice. "Do you remember our talk, mom?"

"Of course I do. Why else would I be all dressed up? It's Charlie that always takes so long. Let me go get him."

"Mom, no. Charlie is not going. It's just you. And we're not going right now; the room is only free next week. We came over to see if you wanted help packing."

"Sure, dear. Where is it I'm going? Do I pack for warmer or cold weather?"

"Not that far, it's the Hummingbird Manor, just a five-minute drive from here. We'll visit often, and they have plenty of activities planned. There's even bingo every week. Some people you know are already there, in rooms right beside you."

I felt another crease begin. I didn't feel old enough to be put into a home, so I refused.

"I thought this would be what you wanted. You didn't mind a few weeks ago."

"You were thinking of this, and didn't ask me? What about my house? A woman shouldn't be made to leave her husband. Who would care for him?"

"Charlie is gone, Phyliss. It's going to be better for you if there are people to help you. We will take care of the house for you. We will take care of everything."

"Where did Charlie go?" I remembered at that point that my husband died the year before but I didn't want to remember. I realized that I did need help but still wasn't ready to admit it.

My daughter was right, although I didn't succumb to that fact until years afterwards.

I passed the years completing crossword puzzles, hiding away in my private room. The nurses brought my breakfast and lunch but forced me to go to the dining room for supper.

The meals were satisfactory but nothing like my homemade meals, when I made them with all the proper ingredients. It was a shame that I wasted so much not having one home to share it. I missed my Charlie.

Julie didn't visit as often as she promised, but I didn't mind. I certainly didn't make the visits pleasant for her when she did come. Every time she left, another wrinkle would visit and insisted on staying. I didn't want to be seen with wrinkles.

She called once and asked if I'd mind if Richard came with her the next day.

"I certainly do. I have bingo tomorrow night, and you're not going to make me miss it."

"Ok, then Friday?"

"If you insist. I guess it would be fine. Don't expect me to make anything for you."

"We don't, mother. And we won't stay long."

She never called to announce her visit, so when I hung up the phone I felt the furrow turn into a permanent crease. I would have cursed Julie for that, but she was my only daughter, so I couldn't no matter how many wrinkles she caused me.

I forgot to go to bingo the next night. I never would admit that to my friends or family, but I did. I guess that I just couldn't recall what day it was. Seems silly, now, I should have been able to remember things like that but such was life.

Julie came with Robert and closed the door once they entered the room. After we made polite conversation, Julie shared the news.

"Mom, I'm pregnant."

"You're what, dear?"

"I'm going to have a baby; Robert and I are going to have a child."

"Good, dear, I'm glad."

"And we wanted to talk about moving into your old house. We haven't been able to sell it yet, so we wanted your consent to move in. It would be the perfect house to raise our family in."

"I'll be happy to share it with you. Are you planning for more?"

"We don't know yet."

I was happy, so happy that I thought a wrinkle may vanish. Who was I kidding? Instead I was blessed with yet another. It seemed no matter the emotion I experienced, another fold would appear.

Soon after, I began forgetting everything. Julie told me the name of her child several times, but it wasn't sticking. On what the nurses referred to as my "good days" I was thankful to even remember my name.

I began joining the others for every meal,

which would pass without anything worth remembering. My life was passing by, and I was telling anyone who would listen to the few stories I remembered. The rest of the time I just made something up. No one ever seemed to notice. Or maybe they didn't care.

PAPER FLOWERS

It was a small box, but it had to be to fit in her doll house; the toys her daddy promised to make for it would be even smaller. Sally had a toy box just like her dolls, and it was already filled with human-sized toys that were formerly her best friends, but the doll house was the object taking up all her time since it was built. Although there was only one doll made so far, it was the only one Sally needed to have to pass the time.

The doll, with its long red hair and fair skin was almost the exact replica of Sally – only the eyes were somehow different. Sally's father explained that no child's eyes should be without light; without joy. He always seemed disappointed when he said this, as if it was his fault her mother died before Sally had the chance to be her daughter. Frank's parents-in-law did blame him, however, as they reasoned if she never became pregnant she would still be alive. The sad part of that was the truth behind it.

Sally named her doll after herself, who was named after her mother. She saw photographs of her mother and realized, at the age of five, that she had her mother's eyes. Frank tried to fix the curse by adding the ingredient of "happy" to the doll's eyes by filling them with sparkles. Frank entered his daughter's room with a few surprises in his pockets.

"Daddy, how are you? I was just about to give Sally a bath, but she would prefer to wait anyway. I'm glad you have come to visit."

"I'm great, Pumpkin, and you?"

"Sally's lonely," she always talked through her special doll, but Frank refused to understand that.

"Well, I've been working on something to fix that for the past few weeks. I wanted to have Sally's new friends just right before introductions were made." He reached into his pocket and retrieved two new dolls. Sally recognized the female from pictures only the doll's eyes were not the same. The doll's eyes were happy, like little Sally's. The other doll was her father; there was no mistaking that.

"Thank you, daddy, now it's one big happy family."

Frank deeply regretted that the only happy family he was able to provide Sally was with wood and a chisel. He thought of marrying again, more for Sally's sake than his own, but he wouldn't put an unsuspecting woman through his problems; he just felt so alone. He knew that no doll, however perfect, would replace his widow or his daughter's mother, but he was trying. He did not know how to reply to his desperate daughter, so he transferred his gifts to her and left the room in silence.

Sally chose to change the name of the mother doll to something more suiting. "Sally, this is your mother, Angel." She said this as if her father were making the introduction and knew her all along. Each day the story began differently every day in the past, but the five-year-old decided to begin one final story now that she had an entire family.

"Mommy, daddy, at last you're both here. Mom, I missed you so much. I have so much planned for us to do. We have mix for cookies, paper, and glue, or we can go outside to play. I have plenty of books for you to read me, but they can wait for bed time if you prefer."

"I haven't made cookies in years; let's do that Sally."

And so the dolls made cookies and cakes and pies until all the flour was used up, and the family had enough food to host a party for five hundred. When she was done playing for the day and Frank went to tuck his daughter in for bed, Sally decided it was a good time to ask.

"Daddy, can my friends have neighbours and a swing set? Mommy says she just loves to swing in her garden."

Frank was silenced by his daughter's words because of how true they were. Lisa loved the country but didn't like the idea of being so far away from civilization. Before she was pregnant with their first child, Sally was growing the most beautiful flower garden. When she told Frank she was pregnant, she was swinging on the set he happily built for her. Her face shone brighter at that moment than Frank had ever seen. They were never happier than at that moment.

"Sally, how did you know that your mother loved her garden?" Frank tried to maintain the garden, but, being so busy caring for his little girl, it was grown over with weeds and the beauty of the garden no longer existed.

"Mommy told me. Are you mad?"

"Oh, not at all, Sweetie. I'm just very surprised. Of course, I will build you a swing set, for your dolls and for you. I'll get started on the neighbours right away."

"Thank you, I'll tell mom in the morning. She'll be so happy."

"You sleep now, OK?"

Without another word Frank's daughter's eyes were closed, and she was snoring before he reached the door. He took one final glance at Sally before turning off the lights and said a prayer in silence. He went downstairs, poured himself a cup of coffee, and went to his garage to begin work on a miniature swing set. Only when it was complete did Frank retire to his room.

Frank awoke to his daughter's laughter coming from the next room. Before he went to visit her, he collected the swing set with hopes that his daughter would love it as much as he and her mother did. He put his hands behind his back after he knocked on Sally's door.

"Good morning, Daddy. Look what Sally and her mother did already. Isn't it beautiful?" Sally pointed to a garden filled with tiny paper flowers; perfect tiny roses and violets that could only possibly be created with tiny hands. Frank set the swing set down exactly where it used to be and sat on his daughter's bed. He watched as Sally placed the mother doll on the swing, as she sat the daughter on the father's knee as they watched the woman swing and Frank began to cry. Sally stood and went to her father after giving the doll one final push.

"Daddy, what's wrong? Did you want to play with me? I don't mind."

"Sally, come here." Frank sat his child on his knee and began a conversation he never thought he'd have to have. "Sally, how did you know about the garden and the swing set?"

"Angel told me. That's what I changed the mommy doll's name to so I wouldn't mix them up. Of course, little Sally's father's name stayed as Frank."

"How did Angel tell you?"

"She talks to me; she also told me to tell you that she's happy. She promises to watch over us and keep us out of trouble. She thinks you're doing a wonderful job with your wood-working but needs you to always remember to wear your safety glasses." A light came into her eyes as she spoke, and Frank was convinced.

Frank hugged his daughter and knew that he was embracing all Sallys. He left his daughter playing with the dolls, returned to the garage, where he put on his glasses, and, through misty eyes, began to build his daughter some neighbours.

LOST AND FOUND

Walking around the field Ralph was able to reign in all the wandering cattle and begin his proper day. Ralph could never understand how farmhands could forget to do such a simple task as locking the gate, but next time it happened he'd have them round up the cows.

His youngest son, Jamie, was in his care today, as Mrs Ralph Robinson had to take care of errands regarding the other children. Unfortunately, at age ten, there wasn't much Jamie could do, and the work still needed to be done. While rounding up the cows, Ralph felt his only choice was to leave his son with one of the morning farmhands but soon realized the mistake he had made. If Dude couldn't handle the cows, he certainly shouldn't have been left in charge of a young hell raiser.

"Jamie! Jamie?" Ralph was bellowing before the barn was even in sight. Mounting his horse, he galloped as quickly as safety would permit. Adjusting his eyes to the darkness consuming the barn's interior, Ralph did not see a soul on two feet. Tying up his favourite horse and cursing under his breath, Ralph began the tedious and valuable time-consuming task of searching the grounds.

Ralph continued hollering as he searched, hoping that by using sight and sound he'd find his boy quickly. With no one in the barn in which he left his son, Ralph ventured outside where he ran into Dude's brother Bill, who was gathering eggs from the chicken coop.

"Bill, have you seen Dude? He has my son, and I can't find either of them."

"Don't know, sir, haven't seen no one for hours but these chickens. Mighty fine chickens, but they don't talk back. Guess it's a good thing."

"Yes, Bill, that's great," his search continued. Walking inside the next barn its stench quickly told him no one would be inside it unless being paid to be. He did see someone inside but knew from his size that it wasn't who he was looking for – Dude stood six feet tall, the tallest of the farm hands.

Checking his watch, Ralph quickly calculated that he was three tasks behind and closing in on the time his wife expected to be back. Ralph knew he would have to find Jamie before she returned.

Wasting time with backtracking, Ralph

knew by getting the horse again he'd be able to make up that time. Not bothering with a saddle or reins, he mounted the horse and was quickly back on track. The next few farmhands he came across were of no use, and the farmer was getting frustrated. With his deep voice resonating to the far corners of his property, Ralph kept his eyes peeled for anyone approaching. Only able to stay in one place for a second, he searched the land with no success.

"Damn it, Dude, where are you?"

"Sir, my name is Jessie. Dude's busy entertaining your son. Are you able to help me; without Dude I'm running behind?"

"You'll be on your own for a while if that man doesn't get back here with my son. Do you know where they went?"

"Sir, I don't Sir. What do you mean I'll be alone? Is Dude in trouble?"

"Never you mind. If you see the two, tell them I need them pronto."

"Will do, Sir, and please do the same for me."

His watch gave him the bad news, and he knew that his wife was well overdue. The only choice Ralph had was to return home and confess. Tying his horse to the picket fence, Ralph dragged his sorry feet to the porch and in the open door. His wife was in the kitchen already baking up a storm, her face so pretty and unworrying.

"Dear, I have a confession..."

"You smelled the pie and came for some, leaving extra chores to the help? I'll forgive you, but the pie isn't ready yet. You look tired. Have a seat, and I'll get you some of that juice you like."

"Dear, listen to me," at the gentle grasp of her hands and the quiet voice Sharon knew something was more wrong than she thought. "I searched everywhere as soon as I realized what happened but I couldn't find him."

"Who, Dear? Did you lose one of the cows?"

Just as Ralph's mouth formed the word he dreaded to say, he saw an image run by the door. He got to his feet quicker than butter melted in the microwave and ran out the front. Glancing to his right, Ralph saw what he spent his precious morning looking for, "Jamie!"

"Yeah. Dad?"

"Where have you been?"

"Playing with Dude. He's great dad.

Thanks for choosing him to look after me."

Not wanting to deal with it, he sent his son inside and went back to work. All day he stewed about Dude's actions and decided, despite his son's loving words, that Dude's actions were inexcusable and he needed to be reprimanded for them.

As soon as he returned for supper, Ralph was set to call his employee but bumped into him instead. "Dude, you've been done for hours. What are you doing walking around the house?"

"Sorry, sir, Jamie invited me to play, and I didn't see any harm in staying. He's a good boy, you must be proud." And then Dude was gone, leaving Ralph speechless. He decided to wait to make the call after his belly was filled with good home cooking. During supper the family noticed that Jamie had a hard time keeping his eyes open. With only a few bites down, he excused himself politely and retired to bed.

After finishing up, both parents went to their youngest son's room to find him sleeping soundly, something he hadn't done for years. Ralph and his wife shared a knowing glance, and Ralph left to call Dude.

"Hello, Dude? It's Ralph. I wanted to talk to

you about today."

"I now realize how concerned you must have been. You must have been furious with me, I apologize."

"You certainly make it hard for a man to fire you, Dude, which was the original reason for my call, but I changed my mind. Jamie is sleeping like a bear in winter. We believe that's all *your* doing. To thank you we want to know if you'd rather watch him than work on the farm. The pay wouldn't change, but the hours would."

"Say no more. What time do you need me tomorrow?"

There he stood, like the sparkle at the end of a kaleidoscope, he was there. It was the point in my life that I finally accepted that he left when he returned.

I began running, not being able to reach him soon enough. It was a year since he had left. For a long time my parents told me he was gone. That he was never coming back. I don't think they realized that they lied. They promised never to lie to me.

We embraced, and it all came back. The day at the park, the ice cream, the sleepovers, all the memories brought to life. We hugged until we could hug no more and then sat down. I sat on his knee, as if the year hadn't passed.

"Mommy told me that we'd never see you again. She'll be so happy."

"She probably didn't think it would be so soon. She wouldn't want to see you sad."

I was so excited that I barely heard his words. "Mommy was just beside me. Daddy, too." I looked around but could not see anyone.

"Hey, where did they go?"

He turned to me and tried to explain as

gently as he could. "They are still where you left them."

"But I didn't leave, Grampie. Why are you being so silly?"

"You're still so young." To no one I could see, I heard him ask why it happened. Why life was so unfair. When he turned to me, I could see a tear fall from his eye.

"Don't be sad, Grampie. We're together again."

"Together forever, sweetie. I'm not sad, just confused." He told me that it was time to talk. He said that I would soon be meeting someone who would clear things up for me. "I want to tell you a few things first."

"Grampie, you sound serious. Am I in trouble?"

"No, no Sweetie. You've always been the perfect little angel. Do you remember what mommy told you when she took you to the hospital?"

At first I thought I was mixed up in the time. Grampie was gone before I got sick. His words brought back the memories of pain, and then I realized something. My stomach didn't hurt. I was wide awake, not dreaming. The vision of

Mommy and Daddy at my bedside, crying. It all played out in my mind.

When I lifted my head, Grampie was gone again. What would be the last tear of sadness began to fall. It was filled with memories, regrets, confusion, and hurt.

A hand reached out before the tear could fall. A gentle touch wiped the tear away.

IDENTITY THEFT

My captor locked me into a damp room with nothing but the clothes on my back and a comb in my pocket. Although I doubted the comb would be any use, I decided not to give it up or let it be known that it was in my possession. I was left to my own devices and used them to try to first figure out the reason why I was captured and how I was to get out. Someone had joined me, but it took a while for my eyes to adjust to see who I assumed was my captor.

"Are you ready to talk now?" he growled.

"I already told you that I am more than willing to talk, but I don't know what you want me to say." I decided to play the role of smart ass. I had a lot to lose but thought it might put the goons off their game, assuming they expected me to cower. Unfortunately, it didn't seem to be working, so I back pedaled; turning the tables.

"Are you ready to tell me what you want? I'd like to know where I am, why I'm here, and what you want to know."

With a kick to my ribs, he explained that I would be watched until I crumbled. The door of my chambers would not be locked, but if I chose to open it, it would be only to talk. It took all the strength I had to nod in defeat before he left me.

Hearing the door of my prison slam reminded me of the van door slamming before the van took me away. The goons had been telling me something, but I couldn't make sense of it all, being too distracted from the sudden disruption of my daily walk. In the dungeon, as the words repeated in my head, they began to take on meaning; I wouldn't be seeing my family again for three days unless I came up with something significant to say. I also knew they wouldn't consider my daughter's birthday the next day as important as I did. I quickly concluded that I would be missing her third birthday, which made me very angry, but the only one that could hear me vent was me. I vented as loudly as I could. No one came in to interrupt me. My voice dying was what stopped me from continuing.

The silence in the van was interrupted with the continuation of my captor's spiel and, as I listened to the words, I concentrated more on the sound than the phrases. I failed miserably at recognizing my captor's voice but placed his accent immediately – Irish. I filed that minute detail into my treasure box and reviewed the meaning of the words once more.

"Until you spill what you know, you'll have only the basic necessities to survive. My companions here will deliver what I think you may need, depending on how long you put yourself through this. I suggest you share your knowledge sooner rather than later. I don't have any qualms about breaking every bone in your perfect physique. Whaddya say – you going to talk or let your bones speak for you?"

"I'll sing you whatever song you request, but unfortunately you haven't told me what it is you want to hear." That ended with my first ever kick in the ribs. Being a sensible man, I tried to avoid harsh situations that involved people bigger than me; standing 6'3" above sea level, it was never difficult to do. On this particular day I was surrounded by enough to make a definite impression on my life.

They took the remainder of the drive to my destination to search me; it took so long I thought for sure I'd piss on their hands when they got frighteningly close to my crotch. Thankfully I held it in but thinking about it brought me back to the dark room. I hadn't peed yet, and it suddenly became an urgent matter. I walked until I found the wall then felt around the room until I found the door and opened it. Just as the "chief" warned, there were two new goons standing guard. One of which looked almost exactly like me, but was bald.

"I need the little boy's room," I admitted.

They laughed before declaring that I just came out of my own private facility, and I asked if they were joking. Their laughter ceased, and they turned to me with metal eyes, kicked me back into the room, and shut the door. I succumbed to wetting myself, thankfully stopping to remove my pants before doing so. The stench filled my nose, and it took all my strength to not vomit; deciding that smell would be even worse. I decided against requesting a pillow and used my pants as a pillow instead. I went to the opposite corner of where I had relieved myself, lay down, and tried to sleep. I hoped that if I fell asleep, I would wake up in my own bed with my wife and daughter beside me. I knew I wouldn't, I couldn't even manage to complete the first part of the plan. I stared at the ceiling and tried to piece together a more feasible escape. Brilliantly one began to take shape that felt like it just might work. I took the comb out of my pocket below my head and began combing my hair.

I couldn't start the plan rolling too fast, or it wouldn't work. I eventually fell asleep, not knowing what time it was as they had confiscated my watch and cell phone. I awoke with the same disorientation I felt while falling asleep. I decided that I needed to create a makeshift calendar for my plan to proceed. I looked around and didn't see anything that appeared even remotely useful. I resorted to removing my shirt, tearing it up, and designating one corner of the room for the pieces of fabric. I created a pathetic calendar, but it was a calendar nonetheless.

I decided to remain awake until exhaustion took over. I naturally fell asleep at eleven PM and awoke at six AM. This would be my method of calculating the passing time.

That done, I began to complete as much as my normal exercise routine as possible but ended it quickly. Without an endless supply of water, the routine I created for myself would be deadly. I sat in the corner, my back against the wall, and I waited.

The day passed without any unpleasant surprises, actually without any surprises period. It was the most uneventful day I ever thought could possibly occur. It was both exciting and a blessing when I felt my eyes begin to droop, and I fell asleep.

When I awoke my "next morning," I felt for the comb and brushed my hair before placing a piece of my shirt in the corner. Then I went back to combing my hair before deciding I had a long way to go before my plan would be effective.

The day passed much like the one before but with a lot more hair added to my pile. Looking at its growth, I was easily amused but became anxious as to where to hide it from any curious visitor. Without a better idea I stuffed the pile into my jeans pocket.

Despite my resolve, my thoughts were too often brought to my family. I hoped they were safe and thought, from the sounds of the captor, that no one knew they existed. This eased my mind only a bit; I knew they would be worried sick about me. Hell, I was worried sick, not to mention dehydrated and starving. I have grown accustomed to three meals a day with snacks throughout. The new meal plan definitely did a number to my system, as well as made me appreciate my wife's cooking more than ever.

The third day I was anxious to see people, so I was alert much earlier than I would have liked. I roughed up my hair, made sure the comb and the hair were safely hidden, and resolved to brush my hair after the festivities. Although anxious knowing they'd arrive, I had no idea what to tell them; I grew more nervous as the time passed.

Finally I heard the door open, something slide across the floor, and the door close. I crawled to the foreign object, saw that it was a dog dish filled with water and one which looked (and tasted) like kibble and laughed hysterically at their tactics. I ate what was given to me and waited for the goons to return.

Thankfully, it wasn't that long of a wait before they sent in the bald guy with the nice eyes. He found it delightful that the dishes were emptied. More physical interrogation began. "Talk to us, Doucet, and this will all be over soon."

"Mr Doucet? I know it's dark, but even you should be smart enough to know it's just us in here."

"Denying it won't change a thing, Doucet.

We know who you are. We just need to find out what you know." I wouldn't tell them what they wanted to hear, so he left me with a swollen eye and more broken ribs. He left discouraged, and I sat encouraged but physically defeated.

I began furiously and devotedly running the comb through my vanishing head of hair and determined that I would be bald by the time they returned to feed me again. If they sent in baldy again, I would have to muster enough strength to break his neck. If they didn't send him, whoever entered would see a bald, thinning man and report his findings back to the ring leader. At that point I hoped whatever they thought I knew was important enough to keep me alive and transfer me to a hospital. From there my chances of escape were dramatically higher. Gathering strength was the largest variable in my plan, but since it was probably my last chance of survival I thought I could manage.

On what I counted to be my sixth day of captivity, most of my formally well-groomed hair resided in my pockets. In a desperate attempt to be completely bald, I was pulling out the remaining pieces when my second tray slid across the floor. I ate the meal more out of necessity than hunger. My twin was the one that entered; apparently, he was my designated guardian. I couldn't see if he was surprised by or even noticed my new look, but I didn't have much time to debate that thought. As soon as he bent down to retrieve the tray, which I set at the far end of the room, I thugged him in the back and then snapped his head like I was shown in the movies. It snapped exactly like it did in Hollywood and was thankfully just as easy.

I dragged the crumpled body to the darkest corner of the room, quickly undressed, and then declothed the goon. After dressing in the goon's clothes I realized some variables I never considered. Mainly that his clothes were approximately ten sizes too big for me and that I must have had a black eye. I chose to stuff what I had left of my clothes into my new ones to bulk up. My eye would have to be improvised when called upon. I had to go.

Opening the door and seeing light for the first time in six days, I was easily disorientated. I tried to recover, but the other goon made a snarky comment about my wobble. I mumbled that the guy in there sucker punched me in the eye and that I had to go to the bathroom to clean it up.

None the wiser, he asked if the hostage was any closer to breaking, but I pretended not to hear. Holding myself back from breaking into a run, I discovered an exit sign and followed it. When I was outside, I ran as fast as I ever did in my life. When I finally stopped to take a breath, I realized that I recognized where I was. I picked up my pace again despite the extra bulk and went directly to the police station.

The officers seemed not to believe my story until I showed them the extra clothing and the size of my outer shell. They immediately sent a SWAT team to the warehouse I was held in, and I called my wife. She too was disbelieving until she met me at the station. Never in a million years would anyone else believe the amount of luck, bad and good, I carried with me.

At least one good thing resulted in my capture – I realized I looked good bald, and I had my name changed to avoid another case of mistaken identity as that was something they had right.

The next day the papers reported on the capture of a leading gang member and some associates who were known for committing various local robberies and drug deals. Doucet was free and clear of any suspicions, and was safe at home with his daughter and wife.

MIRAGE

The clerk looked like she was going to cry if I said boo, so I paid for my gas in silence. I exited the store and got into my car. Quickly recalling the long drive ahead of me and not recalling any more rest stops, I drove my car from the pumps and parked. Looking into the mirror in the bathroom, I realized it was my eyes watering and not the clerks. The embarrassment released another flood – about the umpteenth one that day.

Trying to compose myself with his voice still repeating in my eardrums, I couldn't concentrate or make a decision. Those three little words said so quietly but heard so loudly made things so complicated. He knew it was coming, and thought I did too, but he still forced me to leave. I wouldn't have been able to stay there anyway. Our house held too many memories that weren't healthy for me to relive.

I did see the problems coming, but I was in complete denial about the possible solutions. I thought about what to do if it happened, but I never planned for anything. The friend I always depended on when I was in trouble had moved to the opposite side of the country, unrelated to me at least, but now I was starting to think otherwise. George broke the news, and then left me only an hour to decide what to do and to do it. While I packed some of my favourite things and discarded some others, I sorted through all of my feasible possibilities.

I never had a good relationship with my parents, so going home was out of the question. I lost touch with my brother, and my sister was always a bitch. I made only one close friend since marriage, and George became a closer friend to him. I knew that George had enough decency to leave him free and chose another friend to console with, but I couldn't allow myself to do the expected. I had to be alone and knew the right place to go.

"Excuse me, are you alright in there?" I was taking too long, people were waiting, and now I had to face them despite the tears. I opened the door to a crowd and ran past them, into the car and down the road without looking back. Unfortunately I couldn't do the same with the embarrassment of going through a divorce.
It started to pour, but I drove on. I drove up the nearest road to my final destination, but my lights

shown on an intruder sitting where I planned to go. I quickly realized that it was George. The rock by the ocean was his home actually, but I needed to be there. I turned the car back around and decided to drive the hour back into town.

I needed to be alone and knew right where to go. I drove straight through at just over the speed limit, so I was shocked to again see George sitting at the boardwalk where I planned to go.

I made the decision to leave the car anyway and walked down to the river. George didn't pass me on the road coming up, so he wasn't on the rock as I thought. He wasn't physically anywhere I was, but he would be forever with me.

George was going to divorce me on paper, but he could never leave me.

I sat down on the river bed, took off my shoes, and let the waves reach between my toes. I let myself sink further into the muck, be washed away by the tide, fell asleep, and never woke up.

BRAIN TALE

Volume One

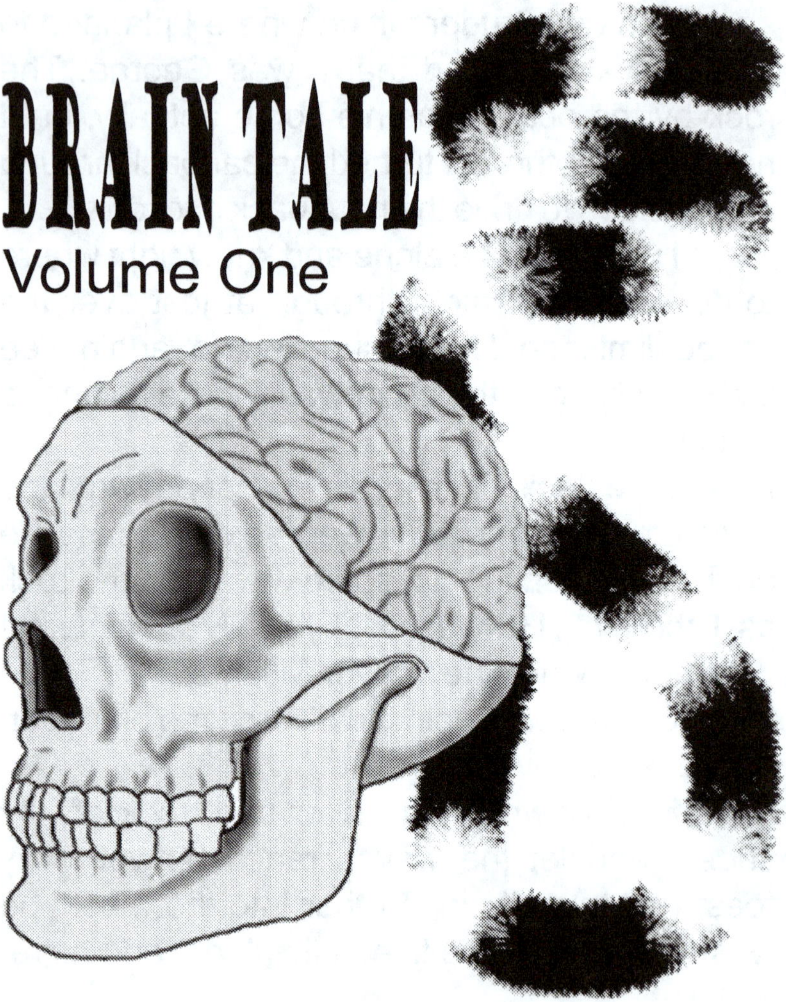

By
Sarah Butland

Visit:
http://www.BrainTales.com
&
http://www.SarahButland.com